Blast Off!

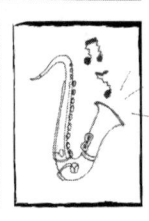

Blast Off!
Carole Bromley

Published 2017 by
Small Donkey Books
The Poetry Business
Bank Street Arts
32-40 Bank Street
Sheffield S1 2DS

Copyright © Carole Bromley 2017
All Rights Reserved

ISBN 978-1-910367-76-6

Designed & typeset by Utter
Printed by CPI Books

Small Donkey Books are a member of Inpress:
www.inpressbooks.co.uk. Distributed by NBN International,
Airport Business Centre, 10 Thornbury Road Plymouth PL 6 7PP

The Poetry Business gratefully acknowledges the support
of Arts Council England.

Contents

9	Down the Cobbled Lane
10	Time Capsule
12	Nature Walk
13	I told a lie on Monday
14	A Dog Called Jack
16	Why?
18	Elijah's Bugs
19	White Horse
20	Who is it?
21	Human Zoo
22	DIY Zoo Poem
23	New Girl
24	Not Wrong, Just Different
25	Under My Bed
26	The Knuckle Down
27	Science
28	Blast Off!
30	School Dinners
32	Caroline and the Scissors
34	Piece of Chalk
36	Poetry Lesson
38	The Six Wives
39	Josephine
40	Instruments of Torture
41	Golden Time

42	Clapping Song
44	Sports Day Blues
46	Test
48	Buddy Bench
49	Geek Family
50	Great Gran's
51	Baby Talk
52	Plug-hole Monster
54	Unsuitable Nursery Rhymes
56	The Little Red Hen
57	The Weather Man
58	Riddles
60	Christmas Angel
62	Weather House
63	The Six O'Clock News
64	There's an alien in my wardrobe
66	Snow Queen
67	Snow White
68	The Wolf
70	Goldilocks
72	Ugly Sister
74	The Princess and the Pea
76	Alice
77	Hansel and Gretel

For my grandchildren

Down the Cobbled Lane

Is where I love to go,
the bumpy way at the terrace backs,
to bang the dustbin lids, chase cats,
scale walls, look over gates
at what I shouldn't know,
that's where I love to go.

Time Capsule

First up was Paul,
with the Berlin Wall

Next comes Mary
Sugarplum Fairy

Martha Nell
brought her favourite shell

Tabitha Grace
her grandmother's face

Elijah Stone
a mobile phone

Mabel Aurelia
an encyclopaedia

Jemima Joy
her favourite toy

Josephine Rose
a clown's red nose

Eleanor Alice
Buckingham Palace

Edward Thomas
tomorrow I promise

Charlotte Vita
a carpet beater

William York
a tuning fork

Oliver James
computer games

Matilda said NO
and wouldn't let go

but Miss said *Look!*
We're a poetry book.

Nature Walk

They all set off in wellies holding hands,
walking in a crocodile. Just half a mile
but Luke dropped behind,
stopped with his bug-pot by some nettles,
got no further. Here's what he found:
one Painted Lady caterpillar,
one black fly with orange legs,
a spider lying in wait on a tense thread,
one late buttercup, one striped feather,
on the underside of a leaf a grasshopper,
one foxglove its seed-pods splitting,
two Cabbage White butterflies dancing
(he didn't try to catch those, just watched them)
and when Miss, a little cross, came back
with her obedient, uninterested herd
she found him, bug-pot full, lying down
counting the spots on a ladybird.

I told a lie on Monday

I told a lie on Monday. Nothing happened,
no-one died, my nose didn't grow
like Pinocchio's.

I told a lie on Tuesday. Nothing happened,
no-one twigged, I hugged my little lie,
sang it a lullaby.

I told a lie on Wednesday. Nothing happened,
No-one found out who broke the TV,
It wasn't me.

I told a lie on Thursday. Nothing happened,
just said *I never touched it.*
Not much.

I told a lie on Friday. Nothing happened,
No homework. What's for supper?
Little fibber.

I told a lie on Saturday. Mum said
I don't believe a word.
Go to bed.

I told the truth on Sunday. No-one heard.

A Dog Called Jack

'*Please*, Mum,' I said,
stroking his silky ear
but Mum looked out the window
as if she couldn't hear.

'*Please*, Mum,' I said,
'I'd walk him every day'
but Mum just pursed her lips
and turned her head away.

'*Please*, Mum,' I said,
kissing his wet, black nose
but Mum just informed me
'We've no room for one of those.'

'*Please*, Mum,' I said,
'he could sleep in my bed.'
but Mum checked her mobile
and firmly shook her head.

'*Please*, Mum,' I said
as he lifted one soft paw.
'You've already got one pet;
we can't keep any more'.

'*Please*, Mum,' I said,
'a gerbil's not the same.
Jack would keep me company;
look, he knows his name!'

'*Please*, Mum,' I said
as the puppy yelped and licked
and gazed at me with big brown eyes.
I was the one he'd picked.

'*Please*, Mum,' I said,
'he loves me, can't you see?
I can't bear to part with him.
He belongs to me.'

'*Please*, Mum,' I said
as she carefully put him back
but we walked home without him,
the dog called Jack.

Why?

Why do people with big angry dogs
say *He won't hurt you?*

Why do people with mangy cats
say *Isn't he beautiful?*

Why do people with boring goldfish
sit and watch them for hours?

Why do people with cockatiels
let them fly round the room?

Why do people with tortoises
think they like being cold?

Why do people with hamsters
wake them up during the day?

Why do people with guinea pigs
treat them like babies?

Why do people with stick insects
keep them in a tank?

Why do people with snakes
insist you hold them?

Why do people with white mice
think they're nice?

Why don't we have any pets?
How about it? Shall we? Yes, let's!

Elijah's Bugs

I don't like people much,
give me bugs any day.
People hurt your feelings
but bugs don't care about that,
they just crawl up your arm
and if it tickles
or they get scared and nip you
they don't mean it.
They're just being bugs.

I always let them go again;
I don't want them to be lonely.
Anyone can be lonely, even a worm
or an earwig or a woodlouse,
they always scuttle or wriggle or fly off
to find a bug just like them
and I watch them and then
knock on Daniel's door
and ask if he's larking.

White Horse

I feel for the horse cut into the hill;
he can't shake his head or twitch his tail.

When somebody steps on that one huge eye,
he can't blink them off like a bothersome fly.

He never will kick up his heels and run;
just lies there all day come rain come sun,

his coat growing yellower, mangy with moss,
the creamy-white mane he never could toss

eroded by weather, by footsteps, by time.
Once thirty-three men lugged six tons of lime

and passed up buckets from hand to hand
creating the biggest horse in the land.

By day you will see him from Leeds or York
that long, white neck, those hooves of chalk;

at night, though, I think of him all alone,
galloping, galloping under the moon.

Who is it?

Who is it, I called.
There was no reply,
just a rush of wings
as an owl flew by.

Who is it, I cried
but there wasn't a word,
just a scuttle of claws
from mouse or bird.

Who are you, I said
to that face in the black
but only the eyes
of an owl looked back.

Human Zoo

I'm a flea
after some tea
watch out for me.

I'm a nit
in your hair. Wash it
don't scratch it!

I'm a thread-worm;
more will come
if you scratch your bum.

These things too
live on you.
You're a human zoo.

DIY Zoo Poem

I went to the zoo and looked in a cage,
>   *Beware of these tigers. They get in a* _ _ _ _

I went to the zoo and looked in the pool.
>   Not a fish in sight, I felt such a _ _ _ _

I went to visit the elephant house.
>   Nothing in there, just a little grey _ _ _ _ _

I followed a sign *This way to the apes.*
>   Not a monkey around to eat my _ _ _ _ _ _

I nagged and nagged to see a giraffe
>   but my father said *You're having a* _ _ _ _ _

they're all fast asleep like the chimpanzees
>   and the sloths and koalas up in the _ _ _ _ _

and the Emperor Penguins in their box,
>   but the owls and the bats and the arctic _ _ _

are all wide awake cos they think it's night,
>   so whatever you do, don't switch on the _ _ _ _ _

New Girl

Everyone wants to be my friend
at first. Everyone wants to know
where I'm from, which road I live in,
whether I have an iPhone 6
and why I'm wearing the wrong colour.

All the girls want to come for tea,
to look in my wardrobe and see
for themselves whether I have
anything interesting to play with,
and eat my Love Hearts.

All the boys want me as a girlfriend
for the first week. They fire arrows
over the hedge with pink scented
envelopes attached to the tip
and say they love me in block capitals.

Then they lose interest
and I'm alone in the playground
kicking a stone while they flick
fidget spinners, skip to unfamiliar chants
and share their sherbet dabs.

Not Wrong, Just Different

There's a line on a map, I've seen it.
To the east all the way from York
to Alnwick people call the little sour fruit
you pick along the railway track
brambles. Say that anywhere west
of the line and they'll laugh
and tell you brambles are the thorns
and the fruit is a blackberry.

For years I thought I was wrong,
that Mrs Anderson and Class Two
were right but now I'll go right on
eating bramble jelly, bramble pie,
bramble crumble; put stewed brambles
on my porridge, bramble jam on my toast,
eat brambles, brambles, brambles
till my lips are stained blue.

Under My Bed

Three shells I found on Whitby beach,
four cherry stones, one mouldy peach,

the spider I didn't want to kill,
some fluff, my walkie-talkie doll,

plimsolls, slippers, outdoor shoes,
a hankie that I never use.

Old Twinkle comics, a sleeping cat,
Di's old lipstick, mum's best hat,

Peter Pan without its cover,
a jigsaw that's not worth the bother,

cornflakes from a midnight feast,
conkers, a hula hoop, a ghost,

the lost key from my brother's train,
that friend I'll never see again.

The Knuckle Down

I didn't know they were playing for keeps
with their glimmers, their bloods, their rubies.

Those swirlies, steelies, aggies and ades
were my friends,

I'd built them homes by cutting doors
in shoe boxes,

tilted the tray so they went in and out
of one another's houses.

Took them to school in a drawstring bag,
chinked them in the pocket of my trousers

at the far edge of a playground
where nobody'd taught me the rules.

I tipped out my tiger, my green ghost that day;
went home with a pocket of commies.

Science

Mr Rossington's hands on the bell-jar
summoned spirits; in rubber tubes
and colourless liquids he held
the secret of life. On Bonfire Night
we gathered round on tall stools
and he dazzled us with pyrotechnics,
the white blaze of magnesium,
a fistful of iron filings turned
into a spitting shower of stars,
earthy sulphur smells rude
as the Grammar School boys
who whistled from the top of the bus
and stuck their tongues out at us
in the glass of the driver's periscope.

Blast Off!

In the corner of my bedroom
it's waiting. *Ten, nine, eight...*
nose-cone pointing skywards
at the ready, till the night

I refuse to do my sums
and mum takes away my iPad.
I run upstairs, slam the door;
it's bleeping on its launch pad.

Quick as a flash it comes to me;
I'll fly it. *Seven, six, five...*
I crouch down in the cardboard box,
I'm clever and I'm brave –

through the roof I'll go, then up,
I know just what to do,
I'm counting down to nothing
four...three...two

one ... ZERO and I'm off,
heading straight for Mars,
steering with my frisbee wheel
past unfamiliar stars,

crash-landing on a cold, white moon
which isn't cheese at all
but stinky socks and apple cores.
I'm hungry and I'm small.

I hear mum's voice. She's calling out
I won't tell you again.
What on earth are you up to? Right!
I'm counting. Eight. Nine.Ten.

School Dinners

I wish I could go home for lunch
and eat a bowl of monster munch.

Instead I wash my hands and queue
with Polly and Louise for stew

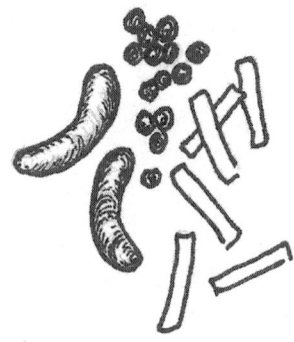

or sausages with beans and chips.
I don't like grapes. I put the pips

around the edges of my dish.
On Fridays when it's always fish

 I cannot stand the little bones
and spit them out like cherry stones.

Grandad says 'When I was small
we didn't have no lunch at all,

we just did sums and learnt to read
and then went home to boiled swede.'

My favourite dinner's pasta bake,
my favourite pudding chocolate cake

but why can't I go home for lunch
and eat a bowl of monster munch?

Caroline and the Scissors

Caroline, Caz to me and you,
was errant daughter number two.
Diana, daughter number one,
it seemed to Caz had all the fun –

she'd scissors that could really cut,
a doll that walked and wee-weed – but
Caz was the sharper of the two
and knew exactly what to do

to put her sister in her place.
She took the doll and inked its face,
she tried to make it run, instead
it wee-weed on Diana's bed.

That night, sent up to bed too early,
she stole the scissors. Her hair was curly;
she cut it all off, *snip, snip, snip* –
oh that would teach Her Ladyship –

and then she snipped her counterpane.
It felt so good. *Again, again!*
They looked for something else to eat,
those blades; her gymslip tasted sweet,

her socks and pants were oh so yummy.
Next day, in trouble with her mummy,
she wished she hadn't. Mum was sad
but that was nothing to her dad;

her parents were in such despair,
especially about her hair.
Her punishment? To go to school
like that. Oh Caz felt such a fool,

her best friend said she'd got the Moth
and all the boys had such a laugh.
The teacher said *That's quite enough!*
You want to tease your friend? Well, tough.

Not in my class. Here we're kind.
One more word, you'll stay behind.
At times we all give in to spite
but hurting others isn't right.

Piece of Chalk

If I scream on the blackboard
and make all the class cover their ears,
it's only because I'm so bored
of writing out the six times table,
spellings to torture parents with
or *What I did at the weekend*.

I don't know what you did
but here's how my weekend went:
as soon as the door closed
and I was left alone with the goldfish,
a pile of exercise books
and that bag of smelly lost property,

I leapt off the ledge under the board
and started writing what I wanted to.
Some of it was a bit silly to be honest,
Daniel has stinky feet. Alice loves Ruairi.
Miss can't sing in tune. And the Head?
He needs to stop doing that combover.

I like to fill that whole blank, black space
with lovely white words. Words I like
the sound of. Long words. Short words.
Words that are hard to say, words that trip
off your tongue, beautiful words, rude words,
scary words, words you only half understand.

Sometimes, alone with the dripping tap,
the squeaking radiator, the fish's splash
or the soft wup wup of the class guinea pig,
I find myself writing a poem,
a secret poem only I can read,
only I can hear in the empty classroom.

By the time Monday morning comes
I will be ready for work again,
but, if you look carefully, you'll see
I am a little shorter, and if you listen
you might just hear an echo of my poem
which is now just a cloud of dust.

Poetry Lesson

'Choose any animal', the teacher said,
'maybe one you don't like
and listen to his point of view.'

Mary chose a rat, Fred a spider,
Ben a duck-billed platypus
but I thought of the rudest word I knew

and picked a dung beetle
not because I don't like them
but so I could say *poo*.

Miss wasn't amused and sent me
to stand outside the door
where there was nothing to do

so I pulled faces at the others
when her back was turned.
Ben laughed. She threw him out too.

We listed animals we didn't like:
crocodiles, bulls, woodlice, sharks,
wasps, rhinos, the kangaroo.

I said, 'What about seagulls
when they snatch your chips?'
and Ben said, 'What about *you*?'

So I said he was an ape anyway
like the king of the swingers.
He belonged in a zoo.

But just then the head walked by,
looked in at the class writing poems,
said 'What have you been up to?'

So Ben looked a little bit sheepish
and I said 'We've been acting daft'
and he said 'So what should you do?'

And I said 'Say sorry to miss, Sir'
and Ben said 'Not do it again'
and he said 'Gentlemen, after you'

and opened the door to the classroom
where Ben managed two lines about seagulls
and I did a dead good haiku.

The Six Wives

King Henry VIII wanted a son
but none of his wives could give him one
so he got rid of them one by one.

Catherine Aragon was first to go;
he went to the Pope and the Pope said no
but Henry was a stubborn so and so.

Divorced her anyway, chose Anne Boleyn
but she was too flirtatious for him
so Henry gave her neck a trim.

Jane Seymour next and here's a thing
the very next day she was wearing his ring
but she wouldn't live to see the spring

so Anne of Cleves was then lined up
but the king didn't find her cute enough
so he ordered his men to buy her off.

Then Catherine Howard. Lasted a year
and when she didn't produce an heir
the executioner took her by the hair.

Catherine Parr was chosen instead
twenty years younger, quiet, well-bred,
smart enough to keep her head.

Josephine

(written jointly with Josephine Bromley, aged 8)

Nathan, Austin, Sean, Joseph, Beanie and me –
V Perran, Alex, Toma, Bradley and Ruriadh
Football's better than staring at TV –
Pass. Shoot. Score, Corner. Throw it to me!

I like chasing Austin – he's the fastest in the school
but my hero's Lianne Sanderson. She's cool
and Steph Houghton who's always No. 5 like me.
When I grow up that's who I'd like to be.

I don't want to sit indoors and wear silly dresses
not since dad took me to watch the Lionesses
and when they scored we all waved our phones in the air.
Lianne's a rebel. Tattoos and spiky hair.

At playtime I play football with Martha and Jess.
I'd rather wear my kit than a sparkly dress
but when I bonked my nose the coach said (get this)
What happened, Princess?

Instruments of Torture

My mum, not being musical,
bought me a drumkit
and I banged away at it
morning, noon and night
till the man next door
who knows a thing
or two about music
said I should start with a recorder –
it wasn't exactly an order
but still she bought me one
and a book about Big A
Little A, bouncing B.
It just wasn't me.

So the man next door
who knows a thing or two
brought round his guitar,
tried to teach me the Mull of Kintyre
which only has two chords–
one too many for me
so the man next door
who could take no more
said try a triangle
get a flute
keep your hand in with a mandolin
but don't touch those drums!
And my mum, not being musical,
went out and bought a saxophone.
The man next door left home.

Golden Time

I might do a painting, I might read a book,
I might write a poem, I might learn to cook.

I might do some tracing, I might act a play,
I might make a pot with some modelling clay.

I might build some Lego, I might sing a song.
I might do some sums, I might get them wrong.

I might get the guinea pig out of his cage,
I might get dressed up and dance on the stage.

I might make a spaceship and fly up to Mars,
I might switch the lights out and study the stars.

I might make a potion, I might cast a spell
I might make a prince from a frog in a well.

I might explore Africa, might cross the Pole,
might play for England, might score a goal.

I might fly a jet plane, might walk on the moon,
I can do what I want for a whole afternoon.

I might be a Viking, I might be from Rome.
I would rule the world but it's time to go home.

Clapping Song

(written jointly with Jemima Sharpe, aged 7)

My best friend gave me a loom band
my best friend gave me a rope
my best friend gave me a promise
but that was just a joke.

She didn't speak on Monday
she didn't speak all day,
she wouldn't let me play with her
and so I ran away.

Someone told the teacher
who went and told the head.
He went and told my mother
who sent me up to bed.

She said, 'You're not a baby'
she said, 'You mustn't cry'
she said, 'I'll tell your father'
but she didn't tell me why.

I gave my friend the loom band
I gave her back the rope
I gave her back the promise;
that was just a joke.

I found another best friend
I found her in the lane
I found she liked to play with me
and I'll play with her again.

So you can keep your apples
and you can keep your pears
and you can save your kisses
for somebody who cares.

Don't tease me with your loom bands
don't tease me with your rope
don't tease me with your promises.
I don't get the joke.

My new friend doesn't tease me,
she doesn't make me cry,
we've put you in this clapping song
my new best friend and I.

Sports Day Blues

End of term and sports again
Every year I pray for rain

Sports Day blues, Sports Day blues
I've got a bad case of Sports Day blues

Can't run, can't jump, can't skip, can't throw
Can't see why I have to go

Sports Day blues, Sports Day blues
I've got a bad case of Sports Day blues

Four hours outside in the scorching sun,
how can anyone find that fun?

Sports Day blues, Sports Day blues
I've got a bad case of Sports Day blues

Can't leap over hurdles, can't jump in a pit.
If there's a point I'm not getting it.

Sports Day blues, Sports Day blues
I've got a bad case of Sports Day blues

Can't crawl under nets in an obstacle race,
my space hopper goes all over the place.

Sports Day blues, Sports Day blues
I've got a bad case of Sports Day blues

All the others go streaking past.
As for me, I'm always last.

Sports Day blues, Sports Day blues
I've got a bad case of Sports Day blues

They gave us an ice cream. It made me feel sick
Frozen carrot juice on a stick!

Sports Day blues, Sports Day blues
I've got a bad case of Sports Day blues

When they get to the tape I'm still at the start
but Miss says what matters is taking part.

Sports Day blues, Sports Day blues
I've got a bad case of Sports Day blues

'At least you tried. Here's your a sticker.
Next year maybe you'll be quicker.'

Sports Day blues, Sports Day blues
I've got a bad case of Sports Day blues

Test

If you tell me how many people got off the train,
how many got on and how many were left
I can work out how many were on to start with.

I can tell a preposition from an adjective,
I know Henry the Eighth had six wives
and loved none of them.

I know the skin on a glass of water
is called a meniscus, aluminium burns white
and a haiku has seventeen syllables.

I know a crotchet from a quaver,
who won the American election,
that there are eleven in a football team.

I know a tadpole turns into a frog,
a caterpillar into a butterfly
and who will be the next King of England.

I know you mustn't eat laburnum seeds,
that cuckoo pint can kill you
and it's unlucky to walk under a ladder.

I know I can swim two lengths without arm-bands,
I know how to ride a bike,
I know my address and phone number.

I don't know why my granny died
or if her house will still have that special smell
of peppermint and polish and chocolate cake.

Buddy Bench

No-one to play with
in need of a mate,
please come and join me
before it's too late.

I'd like to play Star Wars
I'd like to play chase
I'd like to run round
with a smile on my face.

I've waited all lunchtime
and nobody came.
I could play by myself
but it isn't the same.

My mum says don't worry,
just ask them to tea
but when I suggest it
they just laugh at me.

So please come and join me
before it's too late.
No-one to play with
in need of a mate.

Geek Family

Our mam never asks me where I've been,
just sits on the sofa, glued to the screen.

Dad hasn't time to fix my scooter,
too busy tapping at his old computer.

Our kid doesn't talk when he comes home,
just texts his mates on his mobile phone

and my big sister drives me mad,
playing Solitaire on her new iPad.

If it weren't for the dog I'd go insane;
he's always up for a walk in the rain.

Great Gran's

I love going to great-gran's.
Her house is full of stuff
to play with. Not toys, just stuff.

I like to ride on her tea trolley
round and round
till mum says, *That's enough*.

I like to count the mice
on her old furniture.
She has forty-four!

I like to climb her tree
and hide in the branches
and spy on the man next door.

I like squirting the hose,
I fire it over the fence
or write my name in water.

It doesn't take long to disappear.
Great-gran's very old,
she won't always be here.

Baby Talk

Her first word was NO. She'd use it
for everything, even choose it
when she meant yes. No-one knew
what she wanted. We had to guess.

Then one day she said YES
but it was yes to everything,
tapioca, spinach, a red dress,
YES, she'd shout, YES, YES, YES

Would you like to go for a nap? YES
Shall I switch the telly off? YES
Will you always be a baby?
She thought for a moment and said *Maybe*.

Plug-hole Monster

Tabitha Grace is afraid of the plug hole,
terrified it will swallow her whole.

Scared it will gulp down all the toys,
then come looking for girls and boys.

Its been like this since she was two,
her mum and dad don't know what to do,

her gran says *It's beyond a laugh,*
high time that child got used to the bath.

So dad tries to coax her in with bubbles;
when that doesn't solve poor Tabby's troubles,

he gets a sponge and starts to rub
but Tabitha screams *Look under the tub!*

There's a monster hiding who might get out.
Her dad says *What are you talking about?*

but, to keep her quiet, unscrews the side –
Tabitha's cue to run and hide,

leaving wet footprints on the rug,
begging her mum for a kiss and a hug

He's there. I heard him belch and gurgle
I'm not going anywhere near that plughole.

There, there, says dad, *Don't cry, my flower.*
I'll take out the bath and fit a shower.

Now everyone's happy and everyone's clean,
Tabitha's scared of the washing machine!

Unsuitable Nursery Rhymes

Sing a song of sixpence
pocket full of rye
four and twenty blackbirds
got me in the eye.

Mary, Mary, quite contrary
how does your garden grow?
Same as everyone else's.
Who wants to know?

Little Miss Muffet sat on a tuffet
eating her curds and whey
Along came a spider who sat down beside her
so she smacked him with a tray.

East west
where's your vest?

My mother said
I never should
play with the gipsies
in the wood.
Because I never disobey
I asked them round on Saturday.

Little blue Ben, that lives in the glen
keeps a blue cat and one blue hen
which laid of blue eggs a score and ten;
so his mum put the heating back on again.

How many miles to Babylon?
Three score miles and ten.
Can I get there by candlelight?
Don't be ridiculous. Good night.

Humpty Dumpty sat on a wall,
Humpty took no care at all.
All the king's men came by and said *Tough,
that's what you get for showing off.
Get up, Humpty. Shake a leg.
Anyone for scrambled egg?*

The Little Red Hen

I got the book out but took it back,
that Little Red Hen was a pain in the neck,
rushing around telling tales to the King.
Of course the sky wasn't falling in!

And she drove me nuts in her tidy pinny,
asking for help like a clueless ninny.
No wonder nobody gave her a hand,
she was the boringest hen in Boring Land.
Who will help me sow, reap, bake?
No chance, chuck. We'll have chocolate cake.

The Weather Man

I liked it when the weather man
said something rude.

I liked it when the news-reader
got the giggles.

I liked it when the reporter
didn't notice

the cows were about to
knock him over.

Riddles

One of a crowd,
I was first to get lost,
sold for a pound
and some fairy dust.

A fine long wire
red, brown or black.
Pluck me or cut me,
I will be back.

Long and sharp
I rise from my bed,
your mother might cut me,
your father might clip me,
you sister might file me
and paint me bright red.
When you are nervous
you bite me instead.

I hold everything in,
keep everything out,
turn red in the sun,
grow wet when it's hot
and when you cut me
a river flows out.

I am hard, I am white,
something nobody sees.
Take care you don't break me
when climbing in trees.
When you're old I will shrink,
I'll grow brittle and thin
till they dig a long hole
to keep me in.

Answers: tooth, hair, nail, skin, skeleton

Christmas Angel

Every year they take me out,
dust off my golden dress.
Ask them if I they think I'm good;
they'll certainly say yes.

Under my angelic smile
I'm cross. I'd love to play.
I don't get out much. Once a year
is all. What do you say?

That little girl who gazes up
as if I were a saint
could lift me off this spiky tree.
She'd soon find out I ain't.

If she took off my silly clothes
she'd see I'm just a doll
who'd love to join in messy games
but knows she never will.

At night she dreams we fly away,
make mischief on the moon
play hopscotch on the Milky Way
but morning comes too soon.

On Twelfth Night she lifts me down
oh bless her cotton socks
but no what's this she's getting out?
Don't put me in that box!

Weather House

The couple in the weather house go in and out and in and out;
they've nothing left to talk about.

The lady with the parasol will never put her toe outside
on wet days. If she can't decide

she hovers in the doorway while the gentleman in welly boots
cannot stand the sun and shoots

indoors when she appears and doesn't even stop to greet her;
is that any way to treat her?

But she's as bad and cuts him dead, she never smiles or says hello.
I wonder was it always so?

Or did they once upon a time hold hands and venture out together
and never talk about the weather?

The Six O'Clock News

I see them, hundreds of them in boats
like the one we went fishing on,
their faces like my kid brother's

the day he fell into the pond
only it was OK in the end -
someone stretched out an arm.

And I worry about the hungry boy
and his mother and where they slept
and who stretched out an arm

or if anybody did because now
I see them again, running to catch
trains they don't have tickets for.

There's an alien in my wardrobe

There's an alien in my wardrobe
but don't tell anyone.
He's my secret, like a pet
only more exciting.
I feed him on tin cans
nicked from the recycling.

He hides behind my uniform
and comes out in the dark.
His favourite movie's ET,
he watches with one eye,
jumps up and down
and shouts *Me,me,me.*

Sometimes I read him space books;
he thinks he comes from Mars.
He hides under the duvet
at any scary parts.
I teach him how to moonwalk,
that's when the trouble starts.

He can do it across the ceiling
and up and down the walls
but he leaves green footprints
wherever he goes
and I have no idea
how I'll explain those.

I know one day he'll leave me,
I can't keep him forever.
I'll wake up and he won't be there,
I'll search but he'll be gone.
There's an alien in my wardrobe.
Shh! Don't tell anyone.

Snow Queen

Nothing like Elsa. No long blue gloves
could stop the freeze of her touch.

It gave her a buzz to aim that sliver of ice
into my brother's heart. Warned him twice

but he was a dope, wouldn't be told
and once he was in the Snow Queen's hold

he paid no heed to me sprinting after,
I was the tiresome kid sister

and he was the big man riding North
to her glittering home at the ends of the Earth.

I rescued him though. I melted his heart.
I hated it when we were apart.

I keep him close. I guard the key
in case she tempts him away from me

for even though she brought us sorrow
I fear he'd do the same tomorrow.

Snow White

I've nothing against little men
and there's safety in numbers.
Seven felt about right.
All day I'd the house to myself
and a girl needs her space.
I had to promise not to open the door
but that was a small price.

Every morning they'd be off,
hi-hoeing down the path
with their shovels and picks.
The chairs were a tad snug,
it was like living in a doll's house
but I was happy, I was safe,
I was singing all day long

till I opened the window
to the witch, took an apple,
bit into it. You know how it went.
The whole prince to the rescue scene.
Still it was better than back home
where people talked to mirrors
and didn't like the answers.

The Wolf

It's not true that I ate the granny;
thought about it but she was too skinny,
so tough she'd have given me wind.
All I did was put her in a cupboard.

The riding hood made me see red
all that ooh Grandma stuff she said
gruff voice, hairy hands, big teeth.
Couldn't she see what was underneath?

And I never tempted her off that path
Flowers? Me? Don't make me laugh.
What I really wanted was those cakes,
that honey, those yummy tray bakes.

I'm allergic to pesky kids in red
and their bony grans. Whatever I did
I didn't deserve that axe,
just wanted to chill out, relax.

The bed was so comfy, the pillow so soft
I put on the nighty, felt a bit daft
but curled up tight for a bit of a kip
when little red turns up, skippety skip

with marigolds in a little posy.
Why did she have to be so nosy?
Ooh Grandma this Ooh grandma that,
questions, questions. What a brat.

All the better to eat you with. My joke
fell flat. Before you know it this bloke
barges in, never even knocked,
broke the door down. It wasn't locked.

Opened the wardrobe, let out gran,
came at me with his chopper. I ran
in night-cap and bloomers down that lane,
Catch me going there again.

Goldilocks

I'd listened at the door; they were always there,
the daddy with the voice and the enormous chair,
the mummy with the pinny, stirring the vat;
banging his spoon, their spoilt wee brat.

The chance came soon; they were humouring
the kid, swinging him hand to hand,
There there, baby bear let's leave our bowls,
walk in the forest till the porridge cools.

All the more for me; I walked in from the yard
climbed onto daddy's chair - far too hard.
You know the score - hard, soft, right
hot, cold, fine; big, small, mine.

Point was I had the whole place to myself,
put telly on, took a bath, rearranged a shelf.
Then it was Who's been sitting in our chairs,
helping themselves? Beds are for bears

and this one's bust. Yeah, yeah, fair cop.
But they chased after me and didn't stop
till jumping out the window was the only way;
and there's me thinking they'd ask me to stay.

But I'll be back, you mark my words;
bears living in houses! It's just absurd;
bears eating porridge, bears wearing frocks -
next time they're out I'm changing the locks.

Ugly Sister

It's an awful curse having size ten feet,
if you haven't then you should try it.

It's no fun either to have a big nose,
hooked, red, bulbous. One of those –

and tatty hair that looks like straw.
I couldn't stand it any more

especially with Cinders as my kid sis
the sort everybody wants to kiss.

She could have had Buttons after all
no need to steal my Prince at the ball;

he was *mine*, I tell you. In with a chance
till she turns up and he asks her to dance

then she runs away leaving one glass shoe.
Yes, *glass*, I ask you, in size *two*.

The footman called the very next day
so I told Cinders to go and play

and me and Esmeralda had a go
but her heel wouldn't fit and my big toe

got stuck. Then Cinders, all innocent like,
skips in, slips it on. That's all it took.

You know the rest. You've read the book,
how the pretty girls have all the luck

but I'll find a prince who's ten foot tall
with size twelve feet and we'll have a ball.

Prince Charming might be very sweet
but you can't judge a girl by the size of her feet.

The Princess and the Pea

I beat the whole Princess parade.
Not bad for a kitchen maid.

The trick? I knew his mum was dim;
no girl was good enough for him.

That night I turned up at her door
she got more than she bargained for.

Forty mattresses. One dried pea.
An easy-peasy test for me.

Found it at once by candlelight.
Chucked it out. Slept all night.

When she came to say good morning
I was wide awake and yawning;

she asked me *Did you sleep OK?*
I knew exactly what to say;

I didn't sleep a wink, I said,
What is *the matter with this bed?*

Alice

Well, it was hot and I was bored of my sister.
And he did have these long silky ears
so I went. That place was a hole
full of weirdos. Trust me. A nightmare.

You couldn't get a straight answer.
They just sat about on toadstools smoking
or having ridiculous races
or shouting 'Off with their heads'

or grinning till only the grin was left.
Everyone was mad and nobody knew
what time it was. I ate their eat me cake
and I drank their drink me drink,

one minute I couldn't reach the key,
the next I was twenty foot tall
and everybody was running away.
I nearly drowned in a pool of tears

in fact I was lucky to get out alive
and when I did they said I'd been dreaming
and it was still hot and the book my sister
was reading was still boring.

Hansel and Gretel

Crumbs. I'd have used a ball of wool.
Or said I didn't fancy the walk at all.
And I know things were tight
but leaving your kids in the woods isn't right
though your new wife says it's them or you.
You can't let her tell you what to do.
Me and our kid hatched a plan;
sadly it went a little bit wrong.
Or maybe we were just a bit hasty
but that gingerbread house was oh so tasty
with its toffee roof and liquorice door.
We scoffed till we could eat no more
and the witch got us by the scruff of the neck.
We knew then there was no going back.
She fed Hansel up till his buttons popped
and I had to cook and clean till I dropped.
She stoked the fire. It was then that I knew
she was planning to make him into a stew
so I opened the oven and shoved her in;
after all it was her or him,
then I let him out and we both ran home.
Stepmum had gone, dad was alone.
He wasn't all bad. He cried with joy
for his skeletal daughter, his big fat boy.
One grew up, the other grew dafter
and we all lived happily ever after.

About the author and illustrator

Carole Bromley is married with four children and twelve grandchildren. She has two poetry collections for adults, *A Guided Tour of the Ice House* and *The Stonegate Devil*. She was shortlisted for the Manchester Writing for Children Award in 2014 and in 2015 highly commended in the Caterpillar children's poetry competition. Her children's poems have been performed at the CLiPPA awards, published on the Guardian Children's Books website and in Let in the Stars (MMU Publications) and A Poem for Every Night of the Year (MacMillan).

Cathy Benson's drawings and poems for children have appeared in several anthologies. A former teacher, she was born in Scotland, moved to London and now lives in Bradford. Cathy has also published her own collections of poetry for grown ups and has illustrated books by Gerard Benson, including *Ombabalomba* and *How To Catch An Elephant*.

Acknowledgements

Acknowledgements are due to the editors of the following publications where some of these poems have appeared: *Guardian Children's Books website, A Poem for Every Night of the Year* (ed. Allie Esiri, MacMillan), *The Caterpillar* (ed. Rebecca O'Connor), *Fifty Funny Poems for Children* (Thynks Publications), *Let in the Stars* (ed. Mandy Coe, MMU), *The Head that Wears a Crown: Poems about Kings and Queens* (eds. Rachel Piercey and Emma Wright, Emma Press), *English* (OUP), *Three Drops from a Cauldron, Smiths Knoll, ink, sweat and tears, A Bee's Breakfast, Iota, Spilling Cocoa over Martin Amis, Northampton Poetry Competition Anthology, A Guided Tour of the Ice House* (smith|doorstop Books), *The Stonegate Devil* (smith|doorstop Books)

'Goldilocks', 'The Knuckle Down' and 'New Girl' were shortlisted in the Manchester Writing for Children Award 2014. 'Goldilocks' was performed at the CLiPPA awards 2015. 'Hansel and Gretel' was highly commended in the 2016 Caterpillar Competition.

I would also like to thank Cathy Benson for her lovely line drawings, Peter and Ann Sansom for being the best editors ever and George Szirtes, Penelope Shuttle, John Hegley and Rachel Piercey for invaluable advice. The York Stanza group and the Leeds University Poetry Group also gave valuable suggestions on some of these poems.